Contents

Where is Afghanistan?

Afghanistan is a country in south-central Asia. It borders six other countries. Pakistan is to the east and south, while Iran is to the west. To the north are Turkmenistan, Uzbekistan and Tajikistan. It shares a short border with China.

Did you know?

Afghanistan is land-locked. This means it has no coastline.

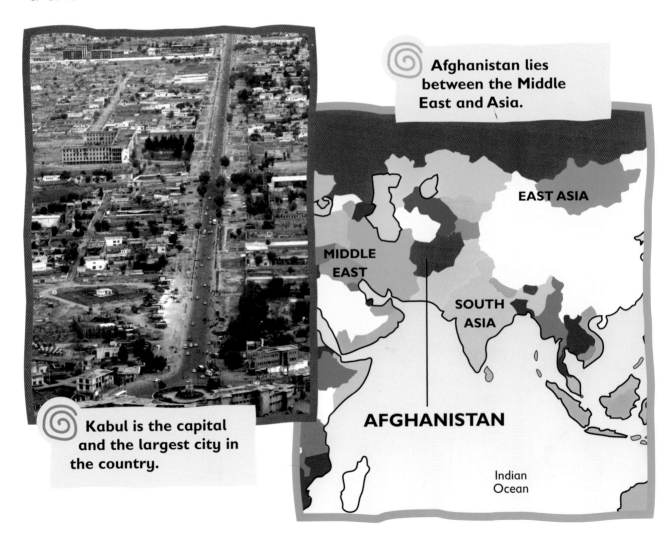

Kabul is the capital and the largest city in the country.

Afghanistan lies between the Middle East and Asia.

EAST ASIA

MIDDLE EAST

SOUTH ASIA

AFGHANISTAN

Indian Ocean

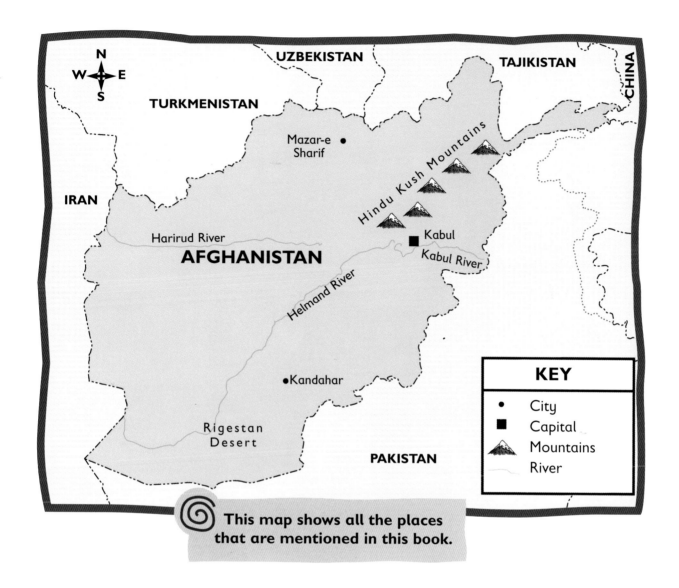

KEY

- City
- Capital
- Mountains
- River

This map shows all the places that are mentioned in this book.

Kabul is the capital. It is in the eastern part of the country, along the Kabul River. Kabul is a very old city, founded more than 3,000 years ago. Kabul was once on the important Silk Road, the trade route between China and Europe. Sadly, many years of war have left parts of this ancient city in ruins and many Afghans are very poor.

The landscape

The Hindu Kush mountain range runs between Afghanistan and Pakistan. The highest peaks are in the north-east. Kabul is in the heart of the mountains. Most Afghans live in the valleys between the mountains.

Did you know?

Earthquakes often occur in the mountains of the north-east. Powerful earthquakes can destroy towns and kill many people.

This photo, taken from the air, shows the bare, steep slopes of the Hindu Kush. Hardly anything will grow there.

The Harirud River provides drinking water for villagers. Farmers also use the river to water their crops.

Rolling hills and high, flat plains called plateaux make up the north. This area is the best for farming, but it is dry. Farmers irrigate their crops from nearby rivers.

Ibex are wild goats with long curved horns. They live in parts of Afghanistan.

The south-western plateau is very dry, with few trees. In the Rigestan Desert, strong winds cause sandstorms. The Helmand River flows south-west from Kabul to the Rigestan Desert. It is the longest river in Afghanistan.

Weather and seasons

Most of Afghanistan is hot and dry in the summer. The south-west is the driest area but more rain falls in the mountains in the east. There, cold winters bring snow from November through to March.

Winter is bitterly cold in Afghanistan. Most people wear coats to keep warm. Some Muslim women wear long body veils or shawls to cover themselves in public.

Desert sandstorms can sweep into villages at high speed. People run for shelter as quickly as they can.

In some years, too much rain falls, making rivers flood. In other years, very little rain falls. Long, dry periods are called droughts. Crops die in the fields and there is not enough food to feed everyone. In a recent drought, millions of Afghans left their homes. Some went to other parts of the country to search for food, others fled to nearby countries for help.

Did you know?

Sandstorms sometimes destroy crops and supplies of clean water. In 2003, huge sandstorms buried whole villages!

Afghan people

Long ago, people travelled along trade roads that crossed Afghanistan. Some of those traders stayed and made the country their home. Almost 32 million people live in Afghanistan. They make up many different ethnic groups. The two biggest groups are the Pashtuns and the Tajiks.

Each group of people has its own language and ways of life. Sometimes the groups fight each other. Fighting among people in the same country is called civil war. There has been civil war in Afghanistan for many years.

Did you know?

Almost half the people in Afghanistan are 15 years old, or younger.

People in Afghanistan use camels to carry heavy loads across the desert.

Afghanistan has two main languages, Dari and Pashto. About half of the people speak Dari. There are many local languages, too.

Muslim boys kneel to pray. Muslims pray five times each day.

The Blue Mosque is in Mazar-e Sharif in northern Afghanistan. It is a holy site and a place of worship for Muslims.

Most people are Muslims, who follow the religion of Islam. Islam has rules about how people should dress and behave outside the home. Some Muslim women wear a long veil called a *burka* when they are in public.

School and family

A group of people called the Taliban ruled Afghanistan from 1996 to 2001. They made people follow very strict Islamic laws. They forbade girls from going to school. Boys mostly attended religious schools.

Did you know?

Most people in Afghanistan cannot read and write. Those who can are mostly men.

After the Taliban lost power, girls were able to go to school. The new government opened more state schools but many children in Afghanistan still do not get an education. More than half the girls do not go to primary school and even fewer go to secondary school.

The Afghan government is trying to help more girls get an education.

A family gathers in front of their house made of sun-dried mud bricks. The father is a shepherd.

A teacher explains a lesson to a young student.

Boys and girls may go to different schools. They start primary school at the age of seven and learn reading, maths and science. They read the Qur'an, the holy book of Islam. Most schools have little money for teachers and books. Many school buildings have been damaged by war. In some areas there are no schools at all.

Grandparents, parents and children often live in the same home. The father is the head of the household. Most mothers cook and care for the family. Some women work outside the home.

Country

Most Afghans live on farms in the countryside. They grow wheat, barley, maize, rice, cotton and opium. Many farmers cannot afford modern tools and machines. Droughts and floods make farming difficult, so lots of farmers can barely feed their families.

Did you know?

Some farmers use qanats to get water to their crops. Qanats collect water from deep underground and then move the water through underground pipes to farm fields.

Oxen pull a plough. Most Afghan farmers do not own modern tools.

Some people in Afghanistan are nomads. They move from place to place to find good land where they can graze their goats or sheep. Nomads live in tents.

© Children care for a herd of goats as the animals graze for food.

© In most villages, women have to fetch and carry water every day for drinking and washing. They carry the water in buckets on their heads.

Years of war have damaged the land and the roads. Most villages do not have electricity or clean drinking water. People are usually very poor and many die from illnesses. There are few places to get good healthcare or education for children.

City

Some Afghans live in cities. Kabul is the biggest city, with a population of about three million people. It is a mixture of tall, new buildings and small mud-brick homes.

Did you know?

Kabul is about 1,800 metres above sea level, making it one of the highest capital cities in the world.

Kabul is a mix of old housing and modern buildings. It has been damaged by years of war. Many areas need to be rebuilt.

People shop in outdoor markets on city streets. The mounds of coloured powder are spices.

The streets of Kabul can become crowded with shoppers.

A lot of city streets are not paved. Few people own cars so they walk to work or ride bikes. Other people take buses or drive carts pulled by horses. Afghanistan's main airport is in Kabul. The country has no trains.

The second-largest city is Kandahar, in the south. It is the main trade centre for sheep, wool, cotton and fruit.

Afghan homes

Most houses in the countryside are made of sun-dried mud bricks. The homes have flat roofs and three or four rooms. Sometimes a mud wall surrounds the house. The wall keeps women from being seen by men outside their families.

Countryside mud brick houses have small windows.

This nomads' tent is made of animal skins and goat hair.

About one in ten Afghans is a nomad. Nomads live in tents that are easy to put up and take down. Camels carry the tents when nomads move from one place to another.

These high-rise flats are being built in Kabul.

In cities, some people live in blocks of flats.

Some people in Afghanistan have had to leave their homes because of war or disasters, such as earthquakes. They live in huts or tents in crowded camps.

Did you know?

Some people have left Afghanistan completely. Many are living in camps in Pakistan.

Food

Most people in Afghanistan grow the food they eat. Women usually cook meals over an open fire. They use flour to make bread called *naan*. People break off pieces of naan to scoop up beef or lamb stew. They also eat a lot of rice. Nuts and fresh fruits are favourite foods, too.

Did you know?

Religious laws do not let Muslims eat pork or other meat from a pig.

Naan is a kind of flatbread. This woman uses her hands to flatten the bread dough.

A boy sells naan on the streets of his village.

Meals are usually served on the floor. People sit on large cushions. Dishes of food are placed on a cloth or a thin mat on the floor or carpet.

Many people in Afghanistan like to drink tea. They sometimes add spices to give the tea more flavour. People visit tea houses to drink tea and chat with friends. Some tea houses are only for men.

These men are chatting over a cup of tea.

At work

Some farmers grow cash crops such as wheat, cotton, fruits, nuts and opium. Cash crops are grown to be sold for money. People export (sell and send) the products to other countries. Wool, rugs and leather are also sold. Weavers make wool into beautiful rugs that are sold around the world.

Did you know?

About eight of every ten people in Afghanistan work in farming.

These women are weaving a traditional rug.

A man sells beads and necklaces at a busy market in Kabul.

A nurse cares for a patient in a health clinic.

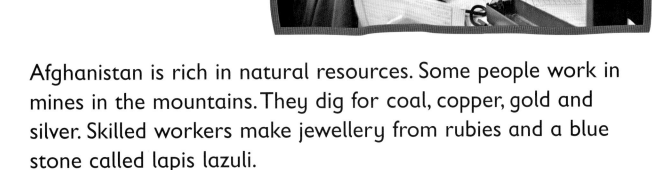

Afghanistan is rich in natural resources. Some people work in mines in the mountains. They dig for coal, copper, gold and silver. Skilled workers make jewellery from rubies and a blue stone called lapis lazuli.

In the cities, people have jobs in shops, restaurants, banks and offices. Some are doctors, nurses or teachers. In Kabul, there are jobs in factories and on building sites. Construction workers fix damaged roads. They also rebuild homes and businesses that were bombed.

Having fun

Few adults in Afghanistan can read, so people often tell folk tales. Parents pass on stories to their children in this way. Many people enjoy folk music and dancing, too. The national dance is called the *attan*. It is often performed at weddings.

Some holidays in Afghanistan are religious. In the holy month of Ramadan, Muslims do not eat or drink during the day. Eid ul-Fitr comes at the end of Ramadan. For three days, people pray, eat special foods and give gifts.

An Afghan girl celebrates Eid ul-Fitr at an amusement park in Kabul.

Buzkashi, the national sport, is hundreds of years old. Two teams of riders compete on horseback. They score points by carrying a headless goat or calf across a goal line. In cities, football and volleyball are popular sports, too.

Boys often make their own kites from pieces of colourful tissue paper and string.

Many boys in Afghanistan like to fly kites. They also play a game called kite-fighting. One player tries to slice another player's kite string. The loser's kite then falls to the ground. In cities, kite shops line the streets.

Did you know?

Kite-flying was not allowed when the Taliban ruled Afghanistan. People could not watch films or the television, or listen to the radio.

Afghanistan: the facts

• Afghanistan is a republic. The country's official name is the Islamic Republic of Afghanistan.

• In 2004, the first democratic presidential elections were held in Afghanistan. Elections for president are held every five years. A president can only be elected twice.

• The United States and other countries sent soldiers to Afghanistan in 2001. The soldiers fight against groups that are enemies of Afghanistan's government.

• People who are 18 or older may vote.

The flag of Afghanistan has three colour bars. They are black, red and green. A central picture shows a mosque, the place of prayer for Muslims.

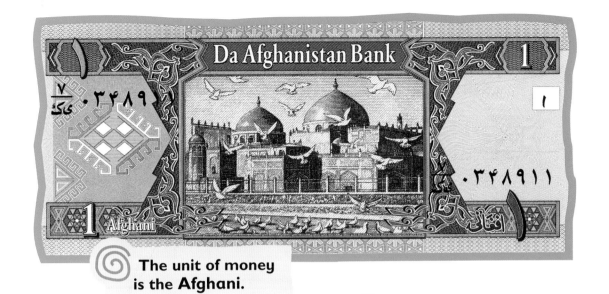

Da Afghanistan Bank

1 Afghani

The unit of money is the **Afghani**.

Years of war have left many parts of Afghanistan in ruins.

Did you know?

Muslims pray at five different times each day. A man called a *muezzin* calls the people to prayer.

• Afghanistan is one of the world's poorest countries. If life is going to get better for its people, Afghanistan will need help from wealthier countries.

Glossary

Afghani the unit of money in Afghanistan.

Burka a long body veil worn by some Afghan women to cover themselves in public.

Cash crops crops, such as wheat or cotton, that are sold for money.

Civil war a war between people within the same country.

Droughts periods of little or no rainfall.

Ethnic group a group of people with the same culture, traditions and way of life.

Export to sell and send products to another country.

Factories buildings where goods are made.

Graze to put animals out to eat grass in fields.

Irrigate to bring water to crops in a field in dry regions.

Islam the religion of Muslims. Islam is based on the teachings of Muhammad (pbuh). The Qur'an is the holy book of Islam.

Mosque an Islamic house of prayer.

Naan a kind of flatbread.

Natural resources things supplied by nature, such as forests and minerals, that are used by people.

Nomads people who move from place to place, living in tents and grazing their animals.

Opium a plant that is grown as a cash crop in Afghanistan. It is made into an illegal drug.

Plateau (plural plateaux) a large area of raised flat land.

Ramadan a holy month observed by Muslims, when they do not eat or drink during daylight hours.

Republic a kind of government in which decisions are made by the people of the country and their elected representatives.

Taliban a very strict Islamic group that controlled Afghanistan from 1996 to 2001 and still fights for control today.

Trade buying and selling of goods by businesses.

Find out more

http://news.bbc.co.uk/cbbcnews/hi/newsid_1650000/newsid_1656100/1656136.stm
The BBC Newsround guide about Afghanistan.

http://news.bbc.co.uk/cbbcnews/hi/newsid_4180000/newsid_4188200/4188287.stm
The BBC Newsround guide about Islam.

www.embassyofafghanistan.org/kids.html
The website for children provided by the Embassy of Afghanistan in Washington, D.C., USA.

Some Afghan words

Pashto and Dari are the two main languages of Afghanistan. They are written using a different alphabet from our own. There are several other languages and many Afghans can speak more than one language.

A few words of Pashto **You say:**	**English**
As-salam-aleikum	Hello
Ho	Yes
Na	No
Ma-na-na	Thank you
Abhaka	Excuse me
Tha tsanga ye?	How are you?
Da khoday-pe-aman	Goodbye

A few words of Dari **You say:**	
Kosh amaded	Welcome
Bale	Yes
Ne/na	No
Lotfan	Please
Tashakor	Thank you
Ma (me) ra bebakhshed	Excuse me
Solh!	Peace!

My map of Afghanistan

Trace this map, colour it in and use the map on page 5 to write the names of all the towns and cities.

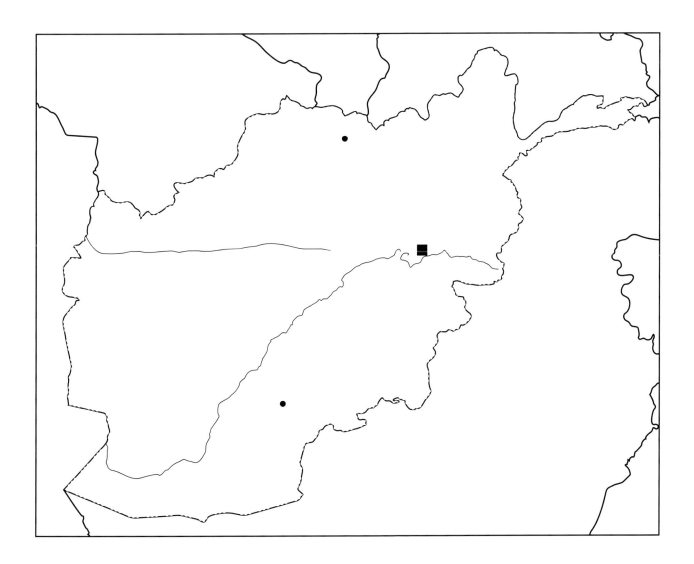

Index

Copyright © 2002 by Nord-Süd Verlag AG, Gossau Zürich, Switzerland
First published in Switzerland under the title *Stimmt das alles was man hört!*
English translation © 2002 by North-South Books Inc., New York

First published in the United States, Great Britain, Canada,
Australia, and New Zealand in 2002 by North-South Books,
an imprint of Nord-Süd Verlag AG, Gossau Zürich, Switzerland.

Distributed in the United States by North-South Books Inc., New York.

Library of Congress Cataloging-in-Publication Data is available.
A CIP catalogue record for this book is available from The British Library.
ISBN 0-7358-1677-8 (trade edition) 10 9 8 7 6 5 4 3 2 1
ISBN 0-7358-1678-6 (library edition) 10 9 8 7 6 5 4 3 2 1

For more information about our books, and the authors and artists
who create them, visit our web site: www.northsouth.com

Printed in Belgium

What Lies on the Other Side?

By Udo Weigelt

Illustrated by Maja Dusíková

Translated by J. Alison James

North-South Books

New York • London

It was a clear, crisp morning after a stormy night. Little Fox was exploring a new part of the woods when he came upon a stream. It wasn't terribly wide, it wasn't too deep, but it was just wide enough and deep enough to stop him from going across.

"I wonder," he said. "I just wonder what it's like on the other side."

"You don't want to go over there!" Squirrel told him.

"Why not?" asked Little Fox.

"Because there's a witch over there who will turn you into a piece of asparagus before you can say *boo!*"

"Have you been there?" asked Little Fox.

"Of course not," said Squirrel. "Much too dangerous."

"Maybe I'd better stay here then," Little Fox said to himself as he continued along the bank of the river. "It sounds scary on the other side."

"You've got that right," said Badger. "A terrible troll lives over there with teeth as big as rocks, and there's a fire-breathing dragon, too!"

"You've been there?" asked Little Fox.

Badger shook his head. "If I had, I wouldn't be here to tell you about it!" he said.

Little Fox nodded and went on.

Just then he saw a raccoon sitting on the other side of the river.

"Hello!" Raccoon
called out. "My, but you are brave!"
"Brave? Why?" asked Little Fox, surprised.
"You're on the dangerous side of the river.
    It's full of nasty robbers, grumpy giants, and
    bloodthirsty knights. I'm surprised you're still
    alive!" Raccoon shivered.
"There's nothing of the sort over here," cried Little Fox.

Then he said, "*You* are the one
who should be afraid! In your woods live
dragons and trolls and witches who turn
you into asparagus before you can say *boo!*"

"But that is not true
at all," Raccoon said amazed.
"Our forest is very lovely, with lots
of friendly animals! Come and see for yourself!"
"I wish I could," said Little Fox. "But how?" He
set out along the bank until he came to a bend
in the river.

There he came upon a tree that must have been knocked down in the storm the night before. It had fallen right across the river. A beaver was already taking limbs and branches to his dam.

Carefully Little Fox stepped across the tree to the other side.

Raccoon met him and took Little Fox around her entire woods. She showed him the prettiest sights and told him all the old stories.

"A long, long time ago," she said, "a witch lived here. She was fond of asparagus and grew a whole field of it. But every night a troll came and stole a few stalks. At last she lost her temper and turned him into a dragon. The troll couldn't fit into his cave as a dragon, so the witch set him

to guard her spell books. Of course, when the witch wasn't looking, he read her spells. And one day he said the magic words and turned the witch into a stalk of asparagus!"

"So that's what happened," said Little Fox, giggling. "And what about the dragon?"

"Oh," said Raccoon, "he flew away. No one knows where. And that's the end of the story." The two animals laughed.

Raccoon came back with Little Fox to his side of the river, and this time Little Fox showed Raccoon the prettiest places and told her all the old stories.

"A long time ago a giant lived there," Little Fox explained, pointing to the ruins of an old castle. "A band of robbers had a camp nearby in the woods.

"One day a knight came into the forest. He wanted to prove himself by slaying the giant and banishing the robbers. The knight had a clever plan. He told the robbers that the giant had a hidden treasure, and then he told the giant that the robbers were plotting to steal the treasure. So the giant and the robbers attacked each other and battled until

they were completely exhausted. Then the knight gathered them up and sent them sailing off in a boat on the river. They've never been heard from since."

"And what happened to the knight?" asked
Raccoon.

"He married a princess and became a king."

Little Fox and Raccoon had a wonderful
afternoon.

The next morning all the animals from both sides of the woods gathered by the fallen log. They had seen Little Fox and Raccoon go across and return safely. Now everyone wanted to try. They ran back and forth to see which side was the loveliest.

There was only one problem. So many animals were trying to cross the tree trunk that a hare nearly fell in the water. So Beaver offered to show the animals how to build a proper bridge.

Everybody pitched in, and the bridge was finished that afternoon. As the sun sank into the forest on Fox's side, and lit the trees on Raccoon's side until they glowed like fire, the animals sat on the bridge and told stories of witches and dragons and giants and trolls, and no one was afraid at all.